THE PRINCESS OF 8TH STREET

LINAS ALSENAS

Abrams Books for Young Readers

New York

Cataloging-in-Publication Data has been
applied for and may be obtained from the Library of Congress
ISBN 978-0-8109-8972-6

Text and illustrations copyright © 2012 Linas Alsenas

Book design by Robyn Ng

Printed and bound in China
10 9 8 7 6 5 4 3 2 1

Abrams Books for Young Readers are available at special discounts when
purchased in quantity for premiums and promotions as well as fundraising or
educational use. Special editions can also be created to specification. For details,
contact specialsales@abramsbooks.com or the address below.

THE ART OF BOOKS SINCE 1949
115 West 18th Street
New York, NY 10011
www.abramsbooks.com

*This book is dedicated
to Felicia Watz,
the Princess of Gräsö*

In a land not far away, in a time not long ago, there was a beautiful princess named Jane.

Princess Jane lived with her royal family high up in a tower, where the princess's bedchamber had a sweeping view over the Kingdom of 8th Street.

Jane knew that being a princess wasn't all parties and games. Her royal duties included keeping up with her studies,

practicing her painting, dancing, and singing,

and managing the royal zoo.

Every day at half past three, Princess Jane would join her ladies-in-waiting for tea. The ladies were very respectful—they never spoke out of turn, and they insisted that the Princess have all the cookies.

But still, the ladies-in-waiting were awfully quiet. Sometimes the Princess felt very lonely.

One day, the Queen entered the Princess's chamber
and asked Jane to accompany her to the market.
Princess Jane was thrilled at the chance to leave the palace.
She excused her ladies-in-waiting, sending one to fetch her cloak.

Suddenly, a horrible toad named Nicholas appeared at the
door and made a nasty face! The toad was always making faces
at Princess Jane, and he tormented her ladies-in-waiting at every
opportunity. Needless to say, he was banned from royal tea parties.

But because she was as good as she was beautiful,
the Princess did not have the loathsome creature squished.
She merely called out to the Queen and watched as the
Queen dragged the scoundrel back to the slimy moat.

Outside the castle, crowds hurried down the thoroughfare, and nobles whisked by in golden carriages.

The Queen took Princess Jane by the hand and led her toward the marketplace.

On the way, the Queen gestured toward the pleasure grounds on the outskirts of their kingdom.

"Would you like to stop here and play for a bit?" she inquired, as she did every time they passed.

The Princess shook her head sadly. She had been to these
pleasure grounds before, and the lords and ladies had not been kind
to her. The Princess was small and delicate, so she could not keep
up with their rough-and-tumble sports.

It was a hard, lonely life being a princess.

At the marketplace, the Queen treated Princess Jane to sweet candies. Although the townspeople must have been surprised to see the Queen and the Princess walking among them, they knew better than to stare at members of the royal family.

After their purchases had been bundled up, the Queen
and the Princess began their journey back to the castle.

As they walked by the pleasure grounds again, the Queen met
a passing noblewoman. They engaged in conversation, and the
Queen insisted that the Princess go off and play while they spoke.

Although she would have preferred to stay with the Queen, the Princess headed into the pleasure grounds. A feeling of dread weighed her down like a stone.

A group of lords and ladies played near the swing set as the Princess lowered herself onto an empty swing.

A young red-haired maiden whom Princess Jane had never seen before approached and asked if the Princess would join their game.

"We're playing tag . . . You're It!" the maiden cried.

Then she ran away. Reluctantly, the Princess
rose from her swing and gave chase to the lords
and ladies.

But as always, the little Princess could not run fast
enough to catch any of them.

Eventually, she collapsed onto a swing, exhausted.
The lords and ladies taunted her: "Ha-ha! You're still It!"

Tired as she was, the Princess had had enough. She defiantly
stuck out her chin (she was a princess, after all) and said, "Yes,
you're right. I am It."

The jeering group fell quiet. They did not know what to make of this royal pronouncement.

The red-haired maiden tapped Jane's shoulder.
"Now *I'm* It!"

Jane replied, "No, I'm still It!"

"No, I'm It!" said the maiden.

The Princess stood. "*I'm* It. I am Jane, the Princess of 8th Street!"

"Well, I'm Samantha, the Princess of 10th Street!"

Princess Jane began to giggle.
Princess Samantha began to laugh.
They decreed they were both It.

Then they chased the lords and ladies about the pleasure
grounds until everyone was out of breath.

From that day onward, Princess Jane and Princess Samantha ruled over the pleasure grounds together.

The Kingdoms of 8th Street and 10th Street were joined in a lasting peace.

A̶nd afternoon tea was never quiet again . . .
especially when the horrid toad tried to join in!

THE END